SYLVIE & TRUE

DAVID McPHAIL

Farrar Straus Giroux

New York

For my girls
Adeline and Kristyn and Kaitlyn
with love from
Papa Dave
(Are you ready to begin?)

Library of Congress Cataloging-in-Publication Data
McPhail, David, date.
    Sylvie and True / David McPhail.— 1st ed.
        p.   cm.
    Summary: Sylvie and her friend True, a giant water snake, share a small
apartment in a big city and have a good time together.
    ISBN-13: 978-0-374-37364-1
    ISBN-10: 0-374-37364-7
    [1. Friendship—Fiction.   2. Snakes—Fiction.   3. City and town life—
Fiction.   4. Humorous stories.]   I. Title.

PZ7.M2427 Syl 2007
[E]—dc22
                                                            2006048979

Contents

Sylvie and True at Home

Sylvie and True lived in a big city.

They shared a small apartment on a quiet street. The apartment had three rooms, plus a bathroom. There was a bedroom, a living room, and a kitchen.

Sylvie had the bedroom all to herself because True slept in the
bathtub.

True was a giant water snake. She liked to fill the tub and sleep with just her nose and tail sticking out of the water.

Behind the apartment was a tiny garden. It reminded True of her old home in the rain forest.

She loved to hide in the thick foliage and surprise Mr. Gomez, their downstairs neighbor.

Mr. Gomez always pretended to be afraid.

"Oh, True," he would say, "you frightened me so!"

"That's because I am a frightful, wild beast," said True.

"You certainly are," said Mr. Gomez, but he couldn't keep from laughing.

True Tries to Cook

Sylvie was a good cook. True was a good eater.

"I'm glad you like to cook," True told Sylvie.

"And I'm glad you like to eat," said Sylvie.

One day, Sylvie called to say she would be working late.
So True decided to surprise her by cooking supper.

She went into the kitchen and looked around. "Hmmm," she
said to herself.

She emptied the food from the refrigerator into a big pot.

She put the pot on the stove, turned it on,

and went into the living room to watch TV.

After a while, the picture was hard to see and True heard a
strange noise. She decided that something must be wrong with the
TV. She was about to call a repair person when Sylvie came home.

"Something's *burning* and the smoke detector is going off!"
Sylvie shouted.

Then True remembered. "I think supper is burning," she said.

Sylvie shut off the stove. True looked into the smoking pot.
"I was trying to cook supper," she said, groaning.

"Thank you for trying," said Sylvie.

Then they opened all the windows and went across the street for pizza while the smoke cleared.

Sylvie and True's Bowling Night

It was Tuesday.

On Tuesdays, True and Sylvie went bowling.

After supper, they put on their bowling shirts, gathered up their bowling balls, and went out.

Sylvie opened the door and walked down the stairs. True
opened the window and slid down the drainpipe. They met on the
sidewalk and headed for the bowling alley.

At the bowling alley they got bowling shoes from Spike, the bowling alley man.

"Size twenty-one, right?" Spike said to True.

"Right," said True. "How did you know?"

"Twenty-one is the biggest size I have," Spike explained, "and you are the only one who ever uses them."

Sylvie bowled first. She knocked down two pins.

Then it was True's turn. She knocked down *all* the pins.

Once, Sylvie protested. "You're over the line," she cried. "That's a *foul!*"

"No, it isn't," True replied, pointing out that her *shoes* were still behind the line.

"I suppose you're right," said Sylvie, sighing.

So every week they bowled . . . and every week True won. But it really didn't matter.

"I had fun," said Sylvie on the way home.

"Me too," said True.

Bedtime

When Sylvie and True got ready for bed, Sylvie put on her colorful pajamas and brushed her teeth.

True didn't wear pajamas because she was already quite colorful, but she did brush her teeth.

While the bathtub was filling, True sat coiled on Sylvie's bed as Sylvie read to her.

"That was a wonderful story," True told Sylvie when she had finished. "Now I am going to sleep."

Then she slithered off to the bathroom and into the tub.

"Good night, Sylvie," True called. "I'm so glad we're friends."

"Me too, True," said Sylvie. "Good night."